EEK!
Stories to make you shriek™

For Beginning Readers
Ages 6-8

This series of spooky stories has been created especially for beginning readers—children in first and second grades who are developing their reading skills.

How do these books help children learn to read?

- Kids love creepy stories and these stories are true page-turners (but never too scary).
- The sentences are short.
- The words are simple and repeated often in the story.
- The type is large with lots of room between words and lines.
- Full-color pictures on every page act as visual "clues" to help children figure out the words on the page.

Once children have read one story, they'll be asking for more!

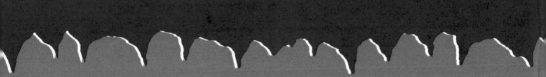

For Pancho and Minnie—J.S.

Library of Congress Cataloging-in-Publication Data

O'Connor, Jane.
        Dragon breath / by Jane O'Connor ; illustrated by Jeff Spackman.
            p.   cm. — (Eek! Stories to make you shriek)
        Audience: Easy-to-read ages 6-8
        Summary: While visiting a town in Wales, a boy encounters a legend of a sleeping dragon that wakes up to ravage the countryside every fifty years, a story that seems about to come true once more.
        [1. Dragons—Fiction. 2. Wales—Fiction.] I. Spackman, Jeff,
ill. II. Title. III. Series.
PZ7.0222Dr 1997
[Fic]—dc20   96-34270
                                                                                                                                CIP
ISBN 0-448-41558-5 (pbk)   B C D E F G H I J   AC

EEK!

Stories to make you shriek™

Dragon Breath

By Jane O'Connor

Illustrated by Jeff Spackman

Grosset & Dunlap • New York

I never wanted to go to Wales for a week. I wanted to go to baseball camp. But my parents said Wales would be great. We were staying in a charming town near a charming castle. And I would make friends with charming Welsh kids.

So in the middle of June, off we went—
by plane, then by train, and then by bus.
A nice old guy named Owen drove us to
Wyllylldrygyn.

Please! Do not ask me how to say it.

The town was not so charming. It smelled bad—like burning rubber. Yuck!

Mom and Dad smelled it too. Owen saw our faces. "It always smells smoky here," he said with a quick smile. "You'll get used to it."

I hoped so.

That night I had to put my hand over my nose to get to sleep. It was the only way to block out the smell.

The next day I borrowed a bike and rode around town. All the people looked at me in a strange way. Like I had no business there. Some welcome!

Just past town near the castle, I saw

some kids playing. KIDS! I rode right over.

I saw girls jumping rope, and girls playing

ball, and some girls climbing a tree. But

there were no boys.

That was strange.

"Who are you? You shouldn't be here!"
a girl said sharply. She looked kind of scared.

"I'm just here for a week," I told her. I
almost added, "Thank goodness!"

"Oh! Just a week," said the girl. "That is
probably all right." She did not look so
scared now.

"My brother has a cap like yours," another girl said.

Her brother! Good! I asked her how old he was.

"Oh, Tim is your age," the girl said. "But he went to Granny's yesterday. All the boys in town are gone. They can't come back until . . ."

The first girl gave her a hard poke. "Hush, Emma! You talk too much."

Then they both ran off. No good-bye or
anything! What a strange, unfriendly town.
A week suddenly seemed like a long time.

The next day I went biking again. There
was nothing else to do. Near the castle, I
saw that old guy—Owen.

"Care for some lunch, lad?" he called to me.

"Sure," I said. At least Owen was friendly.

I parked the bike and sat down. Owen
cut off some cheese and bread for me.
That's when I saw the scar on his hand.
I tried not to stare.

Owen was the keeper of the castle.

"It's called Wyllylldrygyn, same as our town," Owen told me. "It means in the shadow of the dragon."

"Cool!" I said. Then I asked if there really was a dragon.

"Oh, I believe in the dragon. I do indeed, lad," Owen said. "But you are only here for a week. You will not have a chance to find out for yourself. And that is lucky too."

Then Owen stood up quickly. "Now I have been talking too much. And I must get to work."

I asked if I could come back tomorrow.

Owen looked uneasy. "I suppose that will be all right," he finally said.

The next day I met Owen at the castle.
The smoky smell was even stronger here.
Phew!

Still, I had never been in a real castle
before. Some of the walls were gone. And
part of the roof was missing.

But there was lots of armor and shields
and swords. I thought it was cool.

The last room Owen showed me was in
the corner of the castle.

I went no further than the door. The
smell was just awful here. But that wasn't
what made me stop. In front of me was a
giant stone dragon.

Its wings were spread wide open. Its
eyes stared right at me. And they did not
look as if they liked what they saw!

"It—it looks so real," I stammered.

Owen nodded. "It is real to me."

Slowly I walked around the statue of the

dragon. I had never seen anything like it.

I backed away. And as I did, I knocked
over a book. The cover said History of the
Dragon.

I bent down to pick it up. But Owen
took it from me. "There are things in that
book you do not need to know," he said.

I thought over Owen's words that night. What had he meant? What was in that old book? Why wouldn't he . . .

All at once I stopped thinking about Owen. I had something bigger to worry about. The house was shaking like crazy!

"Mom! Dad!" I shouted. "What's going on? Come quick!"

My bed was moving! And the windows
rattled so hard the curtains flapped like
wings.

And then it was over.

"An earthquake?" Mom asked.

"What else?" Dad said.

Let me tell you, none of us got back
to sleep.

Owen called the next morning. "Thank
heavens, you all are safe," he said.

I wanted to find out more about the
earthquake. But all Owen said was, "You
must leave Wyllylldrygyn at once. Things
are happening here much sooner than
they should. It is not safe, lad. For you,
most of all."

I told Dad that Owen said we should leave. And we all agreed. It was time to pack our bags. We had stayed here long enough.

Good-bye, Wyllylldrygyn!

But Owen had been so nice to me. I wanted to see him one last time. I knew Mom and Dad would be mad. So late that afternoon I sneaked outside and rode up to the castle.

"Owen! Owen!" I called out. No answer.
So I went inside.

I walked all over the castle. I even
checked the corner room. But Owen was
not there. Just the dragon.

I knew it was only stone. But its weird

eyes still seemed to stare right at me. It

spooked me out.

And the smoky smell? Well, it wasn't

just a smell anymore. There was <u>real</u>

smoke in the room. My eyes began to water

and sting.

"Owen," I shouted. Still no answer.

I knew I'd better get going. Then I saw
that old book again. It was wrong of me to
open it. But I couldn't stop myself.

I began to read—all alone in the room, just the stone dragon and me.

The book told about the dragon of Wyllylldrygyn. The dragon lay "sleeping inside the rock," the book said. Once every fifty years, on the longest day of the year, the ground shook and trembled. The quake would wake the dragon. It would come roaring out to spread fire over the land until dawn. Then it would return to the rock and sleep for another fifty years.

There was only one way to stop it. A young boy, not yet a man, had to make the dragon see its own face.

Then it would die.

I shut the book. My heart was racing.

The book was saying that there really was

a dragon!

I knew June 21 was the longest day of the year. June 21 was four days away. But there had definitely been a "quake."

Suddenly I remembered what Owen had said about things happening too soon. The dragon was waking up <u>now</u>. That's why all the boys in town had been sent away. Their parents were scared their sons would try to kill the dragon.

That's why Owen wanted me gone too.

Now I am a pretty brave kid. But I am also pretty smart. And I figured I had better get out of this town right away. The book said the dragon was "inside the rock." That probably meant some cave close by.

Then the quake started up again. The ground shook. And I fell.

Stone and dust rained down. I hid under a bench. The stone dragon shook as if it were alive.

Then something happened that I will never forget. Not for as long as I live. The dragon's stone eyes started glowing deep red. Its stone skin turned green and scaly. Its stone jaws opened, and I saw fangs—sharp fangs.

The dragon was not made of stone
anymore!

With every breath, smoke blew out of its

nose and mouth.

I gagged. The terrible smoky smell was

dragon breath!

I struggled to get up. I wanted to run.
But I could not move. It was as if I were
made of stone. Then the dragon stretched
out its long neck and its huge wings.

Stuff came crashing down off the walls.
A silver shield skittered across the floor. I
saw myself in it—I looked like I was
screaming. But no sound came from me.

Then suddenly the shield gave me an idea. It was brilliant! I was brilliant. Maybe I could kill the dragon after all. I would show the dragon its own face, just like the book said.

I was going to be a hero! This town would remember me forever!

The dragon opened its jaws. Out came a stream of fire. I ducked out of the way. Then I grabbed the shield.

Oh no!

The handle was red hot! I screamed and dropped the shield.

The dragon turned. And its mouth

almost seemed to curve into a smile.

Then its great scaly wings thumped on
the floor. It slowly rose into the air. Out it
flew into the black night.

The dragon left behind a trail of fire.
Trees, bushes, grass—everything was in
flames.

The pain in my hand was pretty bad. I felt someone pick me up. It was Owen.

"Oh, lad," he said, "you tried your best. So did I once. Long ago."

Then Owen took me home. He told Mom and Dad a fire had broken out by the castle. And I'd burned my hand.

The next morning, once the fires were put out, Owen drove us to the airport. I remember he waved good-bye. Once again I saw that strange scar on his hand.

All of a sudden I knew just how it had gotten there. Fifty years ago when Owen was a boy, he must have burned himself too, fighting the dragon.

I think about Wyllylldrygyn all the time. The dragon is stone again. It is sleeping deep inside the rock. The next time it comes alive, I will be an old man.

But I bet another boy will try to be a hero. Just like I did.